The Panda Family Relies on Each Other

Short Stories, Fuzzy Animals, and Life Lessons

Karma for Kids Books

Norma MacDonald

The Panda Family Relies on Each Other
Short Stories, Fuzzy Animals, and Life Lessons

Copyright © 2016 Norma MacDonald

First Edition

Published by: Find Your Way Publishing, Inc.
PO BOX 667
Norway, ME 04268 U.S.A.
www.findyourwaypublishing.com

ISBN-13: 978-1-945290-11-4

ISBN-10: 1-945290-11-0

Library of Congress Control Number: 2016960392

Printed in the United States of America.

Dedication

This book is dedicated to all the people trying to make the world a better place. You are making a positive difference!

"Family means no one gets left behind or forgotten." ~ *David Ogden Stiers*

"Karma means you get what you give. You can't hide anything from the Universe. It sees and hears all. What you put out, you will get back. Just like gravity, it's a law of the Universe. The best part about it, is you can have fun with it! What do you want more of? Go give it away. It's that simple." ~ *Unknown*

Table of Contents

About This Book

Welcome to our Karma for Kids Books Series. We are very grateful that you picked up this book. We believe together we can make a positive difference, one child at a time. We strive to instill important life lessons in the lives of young children. We are firm believers in Karma and think that if this simple Law of the Universe is taught to children at a young age, their lives will have the potential to be absolutely amazing.

We once knew a dog named Karma. She was a beautiful, yellow Labrador retriever. It wasn't until after she passed, at 11 years old (God bless her loyal soul.), that we realized just how fitting her name really was.

Karma is indeed a retriever.

Whatever we threw out, Karma was always happy to bring it back to us. It didn't matter what it was, she always brought it back. If we threw out garbage, she'd bring it back without question. If we threw out the most beautiful dog toy, she'd bring it back. It's the same in life. Whatever you send out, is what you will get back. Guaranteed. Every time. Our Karma for Kids Book Series hopes to instill this easy-to-understand Law of the Universe into the lives of children at a young age. The Universe wants to happily bring you all that your heart desires, and it will, effortlessly. But first, you've got to throw out what you want it to bring back to you so that it can! Have fun with this and watch the magic happen. God bless!

Find all of Norma MacDonald's Karma for Kids Books at Amazon.com.

For more of our Karma for Kids books please visit us at:

www.karmaforkidsbooks.wordpress.com
or
www.findyourwaypublishing.com

Other books that we recommend to help children learn important life lessons:

Matt the African Meerkat and Friends: Short Stories, Fuzzy Animals, and Life Lessons by Norma MacDonald

Kimmie Koala and Friends: Short Stories, Fuzzy Animals, and Life Lessons by Norma MacDonald

Cranky Crocodile Saves the Day: Short Stories, Fuzzy Animals, and Life Lessons by Norma MacDonald

The Many Adventures of Peppy the Emperor Penguin: Short Stories, Fuzzy Animals, and Life Lessons by Norma MacDonald

Lucy Llama and Friends: Short Stories, Fuzzy Animals, and Life Lessons by Norma MacDonald

Ethan Eagle and Friends: Short Stories, Fuzzy Animals, and Life Lessons by Norma MacDonald

Billy Brown Bear and Friends: Short Stories, Fuzzy Animals, and Life Lessons by Norma MacDonald

Humble Heron and Friends: Short Stories, Fuzzy Animals, and Life Lessons by Norma MacDonald

Peter Penguin and Friends: Short Stories, Fuzzy Animals and Life Lessons by Norma MacDonald

Guaranteed Success for Kindergarten; 50 Easy Things You Can Do Today! by Marrae Kimball

Guaranteed Success for Grade School; 50 Easy Things You Can Do Today! by Marrae Kimball

The Secret Combination to Middle School: Real Advice from Real Kids, Ideas for Success, and Much More! by Marrae Kimball

The Panda Family Relies on Each Other

Short Stories, Fuzzy Animals, and Life Lessons

Karma for Kids Books

Norma MacDonald

Chapter One

Deep in the tall green mountains of central China, hiding away in large bamboo forests, live the last of the wild giant pandas. Their home is called Sichuan Province, but it's better known by many as the "Home of the Giant Pandas." Altogether, only about 1,600 giant pandas are left up in those mountains. Many people work very hard every day to protect and keep the large black and white bears safe. No one wants to see the giant pandas disappear.

Giant pandas have a big problem. They only eat one kind of food. Bamboo. So, if there's no bamboo, they have no food. And like all creatures here on earth, if they don't have food to eat, they can't stay alive. So many people have been planting bamboo in the forests so that the giant pandas will have enough food to eat forever.

Way up in the highest, most private part of the forest, a small family of giant pandas made their home. There were two child pandas—Min and Ning. This panda family loved to tell stories to each other. Sometimes the stories were true. Sometimes they weren't. That was part of the fun--guessing which stories were true and which weren't. The pandas sat together all day long, munching on bamboo and competing with each other to see who could tell the best story. It was their way of keeping their mind off their big food problem. The family had eaten their way through almost all of the bamboo in the area.

As winter began to set in and the snow began to fall lightly, Min and Ning's parents left the family to search for a place where there was plenty of bamboo to eat. The young pandas four grandparents were in charge of making sure they stayed safe. Min and Ning were super excited because their grandparents were great story tellers. Even better than their parents. But the best storyteller ever was their great uncle, Huan. His name meant happy and he was definitely the most jolly of all the giant pandas. But great Uncle Huan lived far away and they hadn't seen him in a very long time.

Min, whose name meant *clever*, learned much from his grandparents and had become a rather good storyteller himself. His sister, Ning, whose name meant *peaceful*, was not a good storyteller, but she was a very good listener. Their mom's mother and father were named Bao (which meant treasure) and Da (which meant intelligent). Their dad's mother and father were named Jia and Lan— meaning *good* and *orchid*. The young panda's grandparents loved them very much and always tried to make their time together special and fun.

On this particular day, a super chilly wind blew in large flakes of snow. Min and Ning cuddled up with their grandparents who made a tight circle around them and protected them from the worst of the weather. They were all very grateful for their thick black and white fur coats which helped them to stay warm.

As they munched on mostly frozen hard bamboo, Min and Ning grumbled a bit. "We hope our parents find a warmer place for us to live. And we hope they find it soon."

Grandfather Bao smiled at them. "I think maybe it's time for a story, kids. What do you think?"

Both round young panda heads bobbed up and down. "Story. Story. Story!"

"Have you ever heard the tale about Jiang? His parents named him *river* and it turns out he lived up to his name. But not in a good way."

Min shook his head. "I don't remember a story about Jiang."

"Me either," said Ning. "Please tell us."

Before he could start, the kids gathered a great big pile of bamboo and put it in the center of their circle so the story wouldn't be interrupted by the need to get more food. When the pile was four feet high, Grandfather Bao got himself settled into a comfortable position and began to tell the story. "The disaster happened just a week after the snow began to melt and the river was running higher than ever. Jiang had been warned to stay away from the water, but he didn't listen."

"If it was so dangerous, Grandfather, why didn't he listen?" asked Min.

"Because Jiang preferred to be alone. He went to a quiet spot by the river every day to get away from all the other pandas."

Ning and Min scratched their heads and their bellies. "Didn't he love his family?"

"He loved them. He just wasn't sociable. He didn't like talking to others. So, every day he went down to the river so that he could be alone and wouldn't have to speak to anyone."

Ning and Min still had a hard time understanding. Why would a panda not want to talk to his family if he loved them? They didn't get it, but they wanted to hear more about Jiang. "So what happened next, Grandfather?"

"Well, the rains had come down hard during the night. The water had melted the snow in the mountains, but all that snowmelt hadn't gotten downstream yet. So, when Jiang saw that the river appeared normal, he sat down in his special spot in the grass close to the water and began to munch on bamboo like he did every day."

"After a while, Jiang got sleepy. So, he curled up for a nap."

Min yawned. "I could use a nap. This story is putting me to sleep."

Ning nudged her brother. "Don't be rude."

Grandfather Bao smiled. "Here's where the story gets good."

Min sat up straight.

"While Jiang was sleeping, the river rose higher and higher. A rush of water came down from the mountains and washed Jiang away!"

Min and Ning gasped "Did he die?"

Grandfather Bao chuckled. "No, he didn't die. But you can imagine how startled he was to wake up bobbing up and down as his big body got carried swiftly downstream!"

"I'd be screaming for help. Did Jiang scream?" asked Min.

Ning took a big bite of bamboo. "Did anyone come to his rescue?"

"They tried, but no one knew how to help him. He was moving way too fast."

Ning shuddered. "So did they ever see him again?"

"Did he die?" Min asked again as she brushed a pile of snow off her shoulder.

"A week went by. Everyone thought Jiang was gone forever. But then one day, this big brown bear waddled into the camp. No one had ever seen a brown bear before. They all scooted away from it in fear. Then the brown bear spoke. It was Jiang!"

"Why was he brown?" asked Ning.

"Mud. He was covered from head to toe in mud."

Min and Ning laughed. They could picture what a big muddy panda must have looked like. "So what happened to Jiang next?"

Grandfather Bao narrowed his eyes. "He learned the hard way that he needed his family. Sometimes it's good to spend time alone, but not all the time. And especially not when your family warns you of danger. We need each other. That's what families are for. We help and protect each other, right?"

Min and Ning's heads bobbed up and down in agreement. "Thanks for the story, Grandfather. We're glad we have all of you here to keep us safe."

"So what do you think, kids? Did this story really happen or not?"

Min and Ning whispered together for a moment, then Ning spoke up. "I think it's a tall tale, Grandfather, but a good one."

"So you think I made it up?" he asked.

"Yep," the kids said in unison.

Grandfather Bao smiled. "Right you are!"

Min and Ning beamed with happiness. They were glad they had a family who loved them and took care of them and told them stories.

Chapter Two

The next morning, the snow had eased up and the sun tried to peak out from behind the clouds. By noon the sun shone brightly and the snow began to melt from the frozen bamboo. Drip. Drip. Drip.

Min and Ning were the first to arrive at the ever-dwindling bamboo patch. They waited and waited and waited. But their grandparents didn't show up.

"Do you think they're still sleeping?" asked Ning.

Min scratched his fluffy ear. "Maybe we should go wake them up."

Just as they were about to go find them, the four grandparents lumbered into the bamboo patch and greeted their grandchildren. "Zaoshang hao! Good morning!"

After a big group hug, the six pandas sat down for another day of eating and storytelling. "Who's turn is it today?" asked Grandfather Bao. He turned to his wife, Da. "I think you've got a story to tell us, don't you?"

Grandmother Da smiled and nudged her husband. "I think I've got one that will keep our minds busy for a while. Whether it's true or not is for the kids to guess later."

"It happened when I was just a tiny little panda, no bigger than that boulder over there," she said, pointing to a rock the size of a beach ball. "That day my twin sister and I were naughty little girls and wandered away from our parents when they weren't looking. We thought we'd hide deep in the bamboo forest and see how long it would take them to find us."

"Sounds like fun," said Min.

"Sounds naughty," said Ning.

"Ning's right," said Grandma Da. "It was very naughty. Because pretty soon we got scared and decided to go back to our parents. But we got turned around and weren't sure which way to go. The more we tried to find our way out of the bamboo forest, the more confused we got."

Min and Ning's eyes got big. "Did you find your way out?"

"No. We got completely lost."

Min and Ning imagined how they must have felt and shuddered. They'd never been lost before, but they'd heard of cubs wandering off and never coming back. "So what happened next?"

"We sat down and whined and croaked until we didn't have voices anymore."

"Did anyone hear you?"

Grandma Da sighed. "No. We waited and waited. But no one came. We were tired and hungry and surrounded by bamboo, so naturally we started eating."

"So did your parents ever find you?" asked Ning.

Min nudged his sister. "Of course they did, silly."

Ning made a face at him. "How do you know?"

"Because Grandma Da is still alive. If their parents never found them, they wouldn't have survived, right?" He looked to his grandmother for confirmation.

Grandma Da swallowed the big bite of bamboo in her mouth. "We might have survived, but our lives would have been very sad without our parents."

Min and Ning thought about their own parents. What if they got lost? What if they never saw them again? Tears came to their eyes.

Grandma Da saw their distress and quickly put her arms around them. "Don't worry. Your parents will come back. They won't get lost. Your parents are very wise."

Min and Ning wiped the tears from their eyes and hugged their grandmother. "So tell us what happened next, grandmother. How long did it take you to find your way out of the bamboo forest?"

Grandma Da closed her eyes for a moment. "Two days later we heard voices crying out our names. It was our aunt and uncle. They took us back home. Our parents were thrilled to see us."

"I'm sure they were," said Ning.

"Did you get in big trouble?" asked Min.

"Big, big, big trouble," said Grandma Da. "Our parents thought we were gone forever. They hadn't slept the whole time we were gone. When they realized we had disappeared, they gathered a group of friends to make a search party. Dozens of pandas had been out searching for us."

"Whoa," Ning and Min said together. "What was your punishment? Did you get spanked?"

"No spanking. In fact, we just got a long talking to."

Min and Ning looked at each other, puzzled. "You didn't get grounded or have privileges taken away or anything?"

Grandma Da frowned. "The punishment was seeing what we'd put our family through."

"That's it?" asked Min. "Seems like you got off easy."

Grandma Da sighed. "Causing my family pain and suffering was the worst possible punishment, Min. Everyone was so upset because of our bad decision."

Min scratched his ear. "I don't get it."

Ning shook her head at her brother. "Your name means clever, Min, but sometimes you're not very smart."

Ning kicked at his sister. "And you think you are so much smarter than me?"

Grandma Da interrupted the argument before it got worse. "Let me see if I can help you both understand."

Min and Ning glared at each other, but they were eager to hear what their grandmother had to say. So, they sat up straighter and listened.

"Which would hurt worse, being spanked or seeing your mother and father cry?"

Ning answered quickly. "Seeing our parents cry. For sure."

Min scrunched up his face. "I'm still confused. What does parents crying have to do with punishment?"

Grandmother Da put a paw on Min's shoulder. "Are you worried about your parents?"

Min nodded.

"What if you thought they were gone forever, that they were never coming home, how would you feel?"

Min's eyes welled up with tears. "That would be horrible!"

"That's how our parents felt when we disappeared. And my sister and I caused them to feel that way because we were playing a joke on them. When we understood what we'd put them through we felt terrible. That was our punishment.

Knowing that we'd made our parents feel horrible. Do you understand now?"

Min thought for a minute. "So it hurt, just like a spanking would, but in a different way?"

"That's it exactly. We caused our parents much pain and that made us hurt inside, in our hearts. It's not good to play pranks that can hurt people."

While Grandma Da spoke, Ning kept nodding her head. When she realized her brother finally understood she felt relieved. Sometimes her brother played jokes that really upset her, and he didn't understand when she cried. He always teased her. She explained it to him. "It's like when you hide in a patch of bamboo and jump out and scare me," she said. "You cause me pain. But you do it to me all the time."

Min shook his head. "But that's different, right Grandma Da?"

"Not really, Min. It may seem like a small thing compared to what my sister and I did, but if we do things to people that we know hurts them, we're not showing love."

Ning nodded in agreement. Her brother lowered his head. "I guess I shouldn't jump out of the bamboo and scare you   anymore."

"That would make me very happy," said Ning. "And thanks for the story Grandma Da. I think it was a true story. It was, wasn't it?"

Grandma Da smiled. "True, but sad story. I hope you've both learned a lesson from my childhood mistake."

Min and Ning thanked their grandmother. "We will try to never cause our parents pain. We just hope they will come home very, very soon."

All four grandparents snuggled up around Min and Ning. "Don't worry too much. They will come home soon. And we will all have good news about a new place to live."

Chapter Three

It had been three days since any snow had fallen. The giant panda family all smiled at the idea that maybe winter was coming to an end. But their smiles had a touch of sadness. Min and Ning's parents still hadn't returned from their bamboo forest scouting trip. Grandpa Jia, who was a very wonderful storyteller, sat down and gathered the two children around him, one on each side.

Min and Ning cuddled up close to their grandfather and chomped on their bamboo. "Tell us a story, Grandpa Jia."

Their grandfather cleared his throat. "You don't really want to hear any of my boring old stories, do you?"

"Please, Grandpa Jia. We do. We do. We do."

Their grandfather chuckled. "Ok. But you need to promise to pay close attention to this one. It's very, very important."

Min and Ning nodded their heads. "We promise."

Grandpa Jia stretched and took a few deep breaths. "Long, long ago, our family was eating and telling stories."

The entire panda family chuckled. Telling stories and eating was what they did every day. Panda life was rarely very exciting.

"So did something happen, Grandpa Jia?" asked Min.

"Patience, Little One. I'm just getting started. Hmmm. Now, where was I? Oh, yes, it was a day much like today. Eating. Talking. Eating. Talking. But then, a huge crashing sound came from deep in the bamboo forest."

"What was it?" asked Ning. "Was it a monster?"

Grandpa Jia chuckled "No, my dear one. It was not a monster. But a monstrous huge group of pandas came out of the forest and ran towards us. Faces full of fear, they rushed up growling, barking, and huffing. It was crazy!"

"What were they saying?"

"They were so panicked; we couldn't understand a word they were saying. It took quite a while for them to settle down and speak. We found out that something terrible had happened."

"What was it?" asked Min, scooting closer to his Grandpa. "What happened to them?"

"We had a hard time understanding them. They told us about huge metal monsters that came early in the morning and were wiping out all the bamboo."

"I knew there were monsters!" said Ning. "What did the monsters do to the pandas?"

Grandpa Jia shook his big black and white head from side to side. "The pandas ran away as soon as they saw the monsters crashing through the forest. They were so scared. Their food supply was destroyed. When they found us, they were tired and hungry. So, we shared our bamboo with them."

"That was a nice thing to do," said Min. "Sharing is caring. That's what Grandma Lan always says."

"That's right, Min. And we shared. But we soon ran into a big problem. There were so many of those pandas. We wanted to help, but we knew if they stayed with us for much longer, our bamboo forest would disappear and none of us would have anything to eat."

"Definitely a big problem," said Min. "So what did you do?"

"We called a meeting. We told the pandas they could stay with us for one week, but then they would have to go find a bamboo forest of their own."

"Were they mad?" asked Ning.

"No. But it turned out we had a bigger problem than we'd bargained for."

Min and Ning continued to munch on their bamboo and questioned their grandfather about the visiting pandas. How many were there? How old were they? Grandpa Jia explained that there were thirty of them--all different ages. And that they had tremendous appetites and that they talked very loud and made big messes. The visiting pandas stayed up late at night and slept until very late in the morning. And they never said please or thank you. After two days with them, Grandpa Jia's family didn't know how they would survive an entire week.

"So did you tell them to go away?" asked Min. He was imagining the large group of pandas eating everything in sight and making a huge mess of their tidy forest home.

Ning nudged her brother. "Of course they didn't. They invited them to stay for a week, so they had to keep that promise, even if they did have bad manners. Am I right, Grandpa Jia?"

"You are right, my peaceful little girl. We made a promise and we needed to keep our word, even though our visitors were being very bad guests."

"If they were being bad guests, you should have made them leave. That's what I would have done," said Ning. "No bad manners allowed. That's what mother always says."

"True," said Grandpa Jia. "Manners are very important. But there were two more important qualities we needed to show in that situation. Can you guess what they were?"

Min and Ning scrunched up their faces as they thought hard about their grandfather's question. After a few minutes, Ning jumped up and answered. "I know. I know. You needed to show love and kindness."

"Very good answer, my dear one. Those are indeed very precious qualities, but they're not the two I was thinking of." Grandpa Jia put a paw on Min's shoulder. "What about you. Do you have any ideas about what sort of qualities you'd need to show if you were faced with trying to help a group of ill-mannered pandas?"

Min scratched his ear. "Patience. I would need to show lots of patience."

"Exactly," said Grandpa Jia. "Patience and endurance."

"What's endurance?" asked Ning.

Grandpa Jia thought for a minute before he answered. "Endurance is coping with a difficult situation without getting angry about it."

"So were you able to be patient with the pandas? Did you show endurance?" asked Min. "Or did you tell them to go away?"

Grandpa Jia laughed. "By the end of the week, we thought maybe it would have been better if we'd told them to go away, but we patiently endured. And in the end, we were glad we did. We led by example."

"Why? What happened?" asked Ning.

Grandpa Jia described the day that the visiting pandas finally left. They had cried and gave huge hugs and in the end, showed that they were very grateful for the kindness they'd been shown. "Doing the right thing always works out in the end. They thanked us and told us that we had taught them a lot," explained Grandpa Jia.

"Was that a true story, Grandpa Jia? I think that it was!" said Min

"Me too," Ning agreed.

"Yes, kids, you are right. That was a true story." Grandpa Jia confirmed.

Min and Ning thought about the story. They decided that if something like that ever happened to them, they would try to be patient and endure, too.

Chapter Four

The rains fell gently during the night. By morning the bamboo forest dripped and glistened in the sunlight. Grandma Lan, who was the chubbiest panda in the forest, sat down and gathered Min and Ning onto her large lap.

"Do I ever have a story for you children this morning!"

The kids snuggled in close and laid their heads on her chest. "Is it a funny story, grandma?" asked Min.

She chuckled. "It's a crazy story. It happened when I was about your age. And whether or not you believe it really happened, I will leave for you to decide. But I learned a very, very, very important lesson. I hope you'll never have to learn the hard way, the way I learned."

The little pandas snuggled closer and waited for her to begin.

Grandma Lan peered into the sky for quite some time before saying a single word. The kids stared up at the sky, wondering what she was looking at.

"Aha," she finally said, pointing at the sky. "There's one right there."

Min and Hing looked up, but all they could see was a big, white line scrawled across the vast blue sky. "What is that stuff, grandma?"

"It's the smelly gas of the giant birds. Can you see that bird way up there?"

Ning bounced up and down with excitement. "I see it! I see it!"

"There's another one," said Min, pointing towards the mountains. "What kind of birds are they? And why are they flying so high up in the air?"

"Well," said Grandma Lan. "You're not going to believe this, but their bellies are full of humans. They eat them."

"No way!" said Ning. "This isn't a true story. You're making it up."

Grandma Lan put her right paw in the air. "I tell no lies. It's the truth. But I warned you that you'll have to decide for yourselves whether or not you choose to believe me."

Ning smiled. "I believe you, grandmother."

Min snorted. "You're making this up. I'm sure of it."

Grandma Lan laughed and handed them some bamboo. "Someday you might find out for yourselves. In the meantime, let me get on with the story."

The young pandas stuffed the bamboo leaves into their mouths. "Go on."

"So one day, we were taking our afternoon nap when a terrible screeching noise broke the silence of the forest."

"What was it?" asked Min.

"It was one of the giant silver birds, falling, falling, falling from the sky! It was coming right towards us!"

"Really?" asked the young pandas. "What did you do? Where you scared?"

Grandma Lan moved her arms like she was running. "We ran and ran and ran as fast as we could, deep into the forest."

The pandas' eyes got big. "Then what happened? Did the giant bird chase you into the forest?"

"We thought it was going to land right on top of us! But then it flew over our heads and crashed into a nearby field. Boom!"

"Did the giant bird die?" asked Ning.

Grandma Lan lowered her voice. "Well, we all crept to the edge of the forest to have a look. And guess what we saw?"

Min and Ning waited for their grandmother to continue.

"The bird wasn't moving, but all the humans in its belly were crawling out!"

"No way!" said Ning. "They weren't dead?"

"No, they weren't dead. But they were hurt. They needed help."

"You didn't help them, did you?" asked Min. Pandas learned early to be very scared of humans. They'd heard terrible stories of young pandas being kidnapped and carried away by humans, never to be seen again.

Grandma Lan nodded. "It was a difficult decision. We knew that getting involved with humans could be dangerous, but when we saw them bleeding and limping, we knew we couldn't leave them."

"So what did you do?"

"We took care of them, of course. We lead them to the water and showed them where they could find food."

"How long did they stay with you?" asked Ning.

"Only for a day. The next morning a different group of humans arrived and rescued them."

"So you never saw them again?" asked Ning.

"Well, that's where the story gets interesting," said Grandma Lan. "It was about a year later that they showed up again."

"Oh no! Did they come back to kidnap the baby pandas?" asked Min.

Grandma Lan smiled. "Not at all! But that's what we were thinking, so when we spotted them we went deep into the forest and hid."

Min and Ning leaned forward. "What happened next?"

"Well, as we watched from a distance, we noticed them doing something quite peculiar. They were putting thousands and thousands of sticks into the ground."

Min and Ning scrunched up their faces in confusion. "Why were they doing that?"

Grandma smiled. "They were paying us back for the kindness we showed them. They were planting a new bamboo forest."

"Really?" asked Min, taking a bite of bamboo. "I didn't know humans did nice things for pandas."

"They sure did. In fact, that food you're eating right now was planted by those humans."

"No way!" the young pandas said, looking at the food in their hands. "Humans gave us this?"

"They did," said Grandma Lan. "And what does that teach you?"

The young pandas thought for a moment. "Humans aren't as bad I thought," said Min.

Ning agreed. "And if you are helpful, you get helped. Right?"

Grandma Lan hugged them tight. "That's exactly right. Now let's enjoy our breakfast."

So, Min and Ning devoured the delicious bamboo with greater appreciation than ever.

Chapter Five

The sun dipped below the mountains as the winds blew and shifted directions. Min and Ning sensed something was about to change. Were their parents coming back? It had been several weeks since they'd left to find a new food supply. The young pandas began to wonder if they'd ever see their parents again, but they tried not to think about it. That's what their grandparents told them to do. Don't think about it. They'll come back soon. Be patient.

As the sky turned red, orange and yellow, Min shouted in happiness. "Ning, look!" He pointed at a black and white spot moving down the mountain towards them.

Ning squinted. "Do you think it's mother or father?"

"I don't know. Let's go find out," said Min.

The two pandas scooted up the hill as quickly as their little legs would carry them. They scrambled up the path to meet whoever was heading their way. They didn't know if it was a friend or an enemy. Sometimes that was hard to know.

As the giant panda approached, the young pandas squealed in delight. "Uncle Huan!!!"

The elderly panda sat down on his haunches and welcomed the young pandas to sit on his lap. "How are my favorite little bears? Behaving yourselves? I sure hope not!" Uncle Huan chuckled.

Min and Ning snuggled closer. "Have you heard anything about our parents, Uncle Huan? Have you seen them?"

Uncle Huan scratched his ear. "I'm sure they're fine." He looked up toward the mountains. "How about a story to get your mind off your worries?"

The young pandas shook their big black and white heads with eagerness. Uncle Huan was the best storyteller of all.

The sky was quickly darkening and a few bright stars appeared in the vast open sky. A half-moon rose over the mountains. Uncle Huan pointed to a bright red sparkling spot in the sky. "Do you know what that is?" he asked.

"It's a star," said Min.

Ning shook her head. "No. It's a planet."

"Min's right," said Uncle Huan. "It's a star and its name is Aldebaran. But if you look really hard you might be able to see a couple of planets—Mercury and Mars."

Min and Ning squinted, but couldn't see any planets. "Where are they?"

"They're right there." He pointed into the empty sky. "And I'm going to let you in on a little secret, but you've got to promise never to tell anyone."

Min and Ning wiggled in delight. Young pandas loved secrets. Especially secrets from their favorite Uncle. "We'll never, ever, ever tell."

"Promise?"

"Promise." They held up their big paws.

Uncle Huan whispered. "There are little green bears living on those planets. I met them."

"No way!" said Min.

"You're joking, right?" asked Ning.

But both of the young pandas hoped he wasn't. They couldn't wait to hear the rest of the story. "When did you meet them? Where was it?" asked Min. "Can you show us?"

Uncle Huan took a big bite of bamboo and chewed noisily. "It was many, many moons ago on the top of a high mountain, far, far away."

"How did they get there?" asked Ning.

Uncle Huan described a great big round disk, similar to the giant silver birds Grandma Lan told them about. But this round disk didn't have wings. "I was sleeping when I heard a noise like a great big wind. I woke up and saw this thing land on top of the mountain."

"Were you afraid?" asked Ning. "I'd be scared."

Uncle Huan admitted he'd been nervous, but his curiosity had won over his fear. He'd hurried to climb the mountain and investigate. He'd hidden behind a big rock and watched as, one by one, the chubby green bears stepped out of the big silver disk. He thought he was completely invisible behind the rock, but he was wrong. He should have been more careful. Within a minute, one of the green bears spotted him and alerted the others. They rushed towards him.

Ning and Min gasped. "Did you run away?"

"At that moment, I was scared stiff. I couldn't make my legs move."

Min and Ning leaned forward, their eyes wide as saucers. "What happened next, Uncle Huan?"

Their uncle let out a big breath. "They encircled me, grasped my arms and legs, and took me to the big silver disk."

"Did you go inside?" asked Min. "What was it like?"

"I don't remember," said Uncle Huan.

The young pandas let out a big groan of disappointment. They wanted to know what the inside of the space ship looked like. "Try hard, Uncle Huan, you must remember something!"

Uncle Huan shook his head. "All I remember is pink lights and tinkling music and a warm soft bed. When I woke up, I was alone. It didn't take me long to figure out I was on a strange planet. The trees were blue and the grass was bright orange. The green bears and their spaceship were gone."

"Are you serious?" asked Min. "What did you do?"

"The first thing I did was explore. I was hungry and thirsty. Without food and water, I knew I wouldn't survive."

The young pandas wiggled in his lap. They imagined what it must have been like being dumped on a planet alone. "What was it like? What did you find when you went exploring, Uncle?"

"Nothing. Absolutely nothing. At least nothing that I recognized. No bamboo. No water."

"What did you do?"

"I sat down and cried. And then I prayed. For three whole days. And then one morning as I was sleeping, I felt a tap on my shoulder."

The wind ruffled the leaves of the bamboo and the young pandas shuddered. "Who was it? Was it the green bears? Did they come back for you?"

Uncle Huan closed his eyes and took his time responding to the question. In his mind, he was imagining that horribly frightening moment when he opened his eyes and saw a gigantic hairy purple monster hovering over him. He'd screamed and scrambled to his feet, ready to run. But the monster had put his enormous paws on his shoulders. He couldn't move. When he described all of this, Ning's eyes widened. "No way! Did you think the monster was going to eat you?"

"Did you try to punch it? Did you try to fight and get away?" asked Min.

Ning nudged her brother. "Are you crazy? Of course, he didn't punch the monster. You didn't, right Uncle Huan?"

Uncle Huan chuckled. "I was shaking like bamboo during a typhoon. I couldn't punch him if my life depended on it."

The young pandas hammered their uncle with one question after another.

"Hold on. Hold on," he said. "Be patient. I can't answer both of you at once. Let's just continue on with the story, ok?" He gave them a warm smile.

The young pandas nodded. "Ok. We're listening."

"The purple monster had a hungry look in his eyes. At that point, I knew I was a goner. I had no food, no water, and I was under the tight grasp of a hungry beast on a planet somewhere in the middle of the universe with no way to get back home."

"But you're here now. So, something spectacular must have happened," said Min.

Uncle Huan talked about how the purple monster put him on his back and carried him for hours until they finally arrived at the mouth of a dark, soggy cave.

"Then what happened?" asked Min.

Uncle Huan looked at the sun and stood. "Look how late it is. I need to get to bed. I have a long journey tomorrow. I must reach your cousins place before dark."

"What!" both youngsters shouted together. "You can't go until you finish the story."

"I will finish when I return in a couple of weeks. You will just have to be patient and wait."

The young pandas cried out in protest. "That's not fair. We can't wait that long!"

"Patience, my dear ones."

Min and Ning let out big, long sighs. "Please. You can't leave without telling the end of the story."

Uncle Huan scratched his chin. "I've got an idea. How about the two of you work on the end of the story while I'm gone. When I come back you can tell me how you think it ends. Then I will share the true story."

The young pandas looked at each other. Making up the end of the story would give them something to keep their minds off the fact that their parents were gone.

"We'll do it," they said. Patience was hard, but they had no choice. So many things in their lives made them wait. This was just one more thing. Their grandmother had always said, "You won't always get your way, kids. Once you learn this important lesson, life will be peaceful and easier. If you don't learn and accept that we can't always get our way, then life will be frustrating and cause us anger."

This was one of those times. They wanted to hear the rest of the story now, but their uncle needed to get going. They couldn't get their way. They could either accept it and be at peace, or not accept it and be miserable. They chose to accept it and make the best of it. Using their imagination to make up the end of the story would be fun!

Chapter Six

As the days rolled along, the kids grew restless. They found it harder and harder to get enough bamboo to eat. They really, really missed their parents who still hadn't returned. Their grandparents had a hard time convincing them to stay put and not go out searching for their mom and dad. Min and Ning began to give up hope they'd ever see their parents again.

They were feeling so sad, they forgot all about Uncle Huan's suggestion that they tell the end of the green bear and purple monster story. But one night, as they stared at the stars, Ning finally remembered. "How about we finish that crazy story of Uncle Huan's, Min?" She nudged her brother.

Min stared at the stars. "Do you think it's a true story?"

Ning's face scrunched. "I don't believe it. What do you think?"

Her brother agreed. The story was too crazy to be true. Sometimes it was hard to know if others were telling the truth or not--what was real and what was not.

"Where did Uncle Huan leave off?" asked Ning. "I can't remember."

Min closed his eyes for a second. That's what he did when he needed to think. "The purple monster had taken him to a wet cave."

"That's right," said Ning. "I remember now."

The young pandas sat and imagined Uncle Huan at the mouth of a cave with the purple monster. After a minute or two, Ning started the story where Uncle Huan left off. "The purple monster breathed down Uncle Huan's neck. The monster's breath smelled like rotten fish."

"Eww," said Min. "That's gross."

Ning sighed. "Will you let me tell the story without interrupting?"

Min frowned. "Uncle Huan said we should both tell the story. It's my turn."

Ning rolled her eyes. "Go ahead then. We can each tell two sentences, ok?"

"Whatever," said Min. "So the monster roared and beat his chest and dragged Uncle Huan into the dark cave. The floor of the cave was covered with bones."

Ning cringed. "Uncle Huan saw the bones and knew he had to escape. So, he punched the monster in the nose and ran away."

"No he didn't," said Min. "That's too easy."

"But that's what I say happened. I can tell the story however I want," said Ning.

The two young pandas were arguing and didn't notice their friend, Bai, sneaking up behind them. When he touched their backs, and shouted "boo!" Min and Ning jumped two feet in the air. Bai laughed. "Gotcha!"

Min and Ning nudged and scolded him. "You scared us half to death."

Bai chuckled. "You should have seen your faces."

"Besides scaring pandas to death, what have you been doing lately? We haven't seen you in ages. Where've you been?" asked Min.

"You'll never believe me if I tell you," Bai answered.

The young pandas laughed. "We never believe you anyway. Try us. What's your latest wild story?"

Bai's face got serious. "This is a true story. And it's important you believe me." He lowered his voice. "Our lives may depend on it."

Min and Ning looked at each other. They couldn't tell if Bai was telling the truth or not.

They'd hear his story and then decide. "Go ahead," they said.

Bai grabbed a couple of thin, scraggly branches of bamboo and took a few bites before he sat down to speak. What could Bai have to tell them that was a matter of life and death? Did it have to do with their missing parents? Were they in danger?

"It's about food," said Bai. "Everyone knows the bamboo forests have been disappearing. The truth is, all the adult pandas are worried. Your parents left a while back and my parents left last week. Pandas everywhere are searching, but so far they've had no success. If they can't find a fresh and lush bamboo forest, we may all starve to death."

Min and Ning sat in silence. They knew the situation was serious, but they didn't know it was so bad. "What can we do?" asked Min. "It doesn't seem right for us to just sit around waiting. It seems so hopeless."

Ning bowed her head in discouragement. "Maybe there's nothing we can do."

"That's what I want to tell you." Bai's face glowed with excitement. "I found a huge bamboo forest."

Min and Ning's eyes widened. "Are you serious? Where?"

"That's the problem," said Bai. "I can't find it again. I've been trying for days and days. It's like the place just disappeared. Maybe I imagined it. But I don't think so!"

None of them said anything for a few minutes. Then Min stood up. "There's only one way to find out. We need to find that bamboo forest."

Min and Bai agreed to go. But Ning knew that their grandparents would never let them. She mentioned that to Bai and Min, but they weren't worried. "We don't have to tell them. They probably won't even notice we're gone."

But Ning didn't feel good about that. Her grandparents would know and they would be very worried. She couldn't do that to them. "You guys can go, but I'm gonna stay here. I don't have a good feeling about it. I don't think you should go without telling the grownups."

"You're probably right," said Min. "But I still want to go search with Bai. Okay, you can go tell them of our plan. Hopefully we will be back before dark and then tomorrow we can all go to the new place together and eat to our heart's content."

"I sure hope so." Ning confided, as she went in search of their grandparents. As she watched Bai and Min walk into the distance, she had a worried feeling in her tummy. She tried to stay busy by imagining the rest of Uncle Huan's story, but it just wasn't as fun telling a story to herself.

At sunset, Ning began to worry. All day she'd tried to keep buys, but as darkness fell, she began to worry more than ever. Her parents were gone. Now her brother was gone. Would she ever see any of them again? Sadness felt like a rock in her chest. Hopelessness overcame her. Ning went to bed early. She felt no hope of ever seeing her parents or brother again.

Ning had just settled into bed and closed her eyes when she heard a bunch of loud voices. Was that her father's voice or was she dreaming? Ning jumped up and raced into the clearing. She rubbed her eyes. Was she seeing things? Was that really her mother and father and brother? It was! And Uncle Huan was with them, too. Ning felt so relieved.

The Panda family nudged and snuggled each other. Ning had never been so happy in all her life. Then she remembered about the food problem. Had her parents found a new place for them to live and eat? She didn't have to wait long for the answer.

Uncle Huan raised a paw and said a word of thanks. "We are grateful today that our family is united together again and will soon move to a healthy and very large bamboo forest."

The panda family cheered. Hope was restored. Never again would they ever lose hope.

Ning and Min found out that Uncle Huan's story was not real and that it had been inspired by a dream he once had. They shared their endings with him, and all laughed and played and ate bamboo together in their new home.

AFTERWORD

Thanks again for picking up this book! You are participating in making our world a better place.

For more of our *Karma for Kids Books* please visit us at:

www.karmaforkidsbooks.wordpress.com
or
www.findyourwaypublishing.com

Find Norma MacDonald and her books online at Amazon.com.

Matt the African Meerkat and Friends: Short Stories, Fuzzy Animals, and Life Lessons

The Many Adventures of Peppy the Emperor Penguin: Short Stories, Fuzzy Animals, and Life Lessons

Kimmie Koala and Friends: Short Stories, Fuzzy Animals, and Life Lessons

Cranky Crocodile Saves the Day: Short Stories, Fuzzy Animals, and Life Lessons

Lucy Llama and Friends: Short Stories, Fuzzy Animals, and Life Lessons

Ethan the Eagle and Friends; Short Stories, Fuzzy Animals, and Life Lessons

Billy Brown Bear and Friends; Short Stories, Fuzzy Animals, and Life Lessons

Humble Heron and Friends; Short Stories, Fuzzy Animals, and Life Lessons

Peter Penguin and Friends; Short Stories, Fuzzy Animals, and Life Lessons

Other books that we recommend to help children learn important life lessons:

Guaranteed Success for Kindergarten; 50 Easy Things You Can Do Today! by Marrae Kimball

Guaranteed Success for Grade School; 50 Easy Things You Can Do Today! by Marrae Kimball

The Secret Combination to Middle School: Real Advice from Real Kids, Ideas for Success, and Much More! by Marrae Kimball

If you have ideas for stories, please feel free to share
and send them to:

Melissa Eshleman
Find Your Way Publishing, Inc.
PO Box 667
Norway, ME 04268
Melissa@findyourwaypublishing.com

www.findyourwaypublishing.com

Thank you!

Disclaimer

The purpose of this book is for entertainment purposes only. This book is designed to provide information and motivation to our readers. The content of each story is the sole expression and opinion of its author, and not necessarily that of the publisher. Names, characters, businesses, places, and incidents are either the products of the authors' imaginations or used in a fictitious manner. Any resemblance to actual persons, living or dead, businesses, companies, events, locales, or actual events is entirely coincidental. This book is not intended nor is it implied to be a substitute for professional medical advice, and any medical advice and any medical information contained in this book is not intended to be diagnostic or treatment in any way. The author and publisher are not engaged in rendering medical, psychological, legal, or any other professional services. If medical, psychological or other expert assistance is required, please talk to your physician and locate the services of a competent professional. The author and publisher shall have neither liability nor responsibility to any person or entity with respect to any loss or damage caused, or alleged to have been caused, directly or indirectly, by the information contained in this book. Neither the publisher nor the individual author(s) shall be liable for any physical, psychological, emotional, financial, or commercial damages, including, but not limited to, special, incidental, consequential or other damages. If you do not wish to be bound by the above, you may return this book along with a copy of the receipt to the publisher for a full refund.